ABOUT THE BANK STREET READY-TO-READ SERIES

Seventy years of educational research and innovative teaching have given the Bank Street College of Education the reputation as America's most trusted name in early childhood education.

Because no two children are exactly alike in their development, we have designed the *Bank Street Ready-to-Read* series in three levels to accommodate the individual stages of reading readiness of children ages four through eight.

- ● *Level 1:* GETTING READY TO READ—read-alouds for children who are taking their first steps toward reading.
- ● *Level 2:* READING TOGETHER—for children who are just beginning to read by themselves but may need a little help.
- ○ *Level 3:* I CAN READ IT MYSELF—for children who can read independently.

Our three levels make it easy to select the books most appropriate for a child's development and enable him or her to grow with the series step by step. The *Bank Street Ready-to-Read* books also overlap and reinforce each other, further encouraging the reading process.

We feel that making reading fun and enjoyable is the single most important thing that you can do to help children become good readers. And we hope you'll be a part of Bank Street's long tradition of learning through sharing.

The Bank Street College of Education

D0071736

To Nina and David
—S.R.

To Alessandra
—F.T.

THINGS THAT GO:
A TRAVELING ALPHABET
A Bantam Little Rooster Book
Simultaneous paper-over-board and trade paper editions/April 1990

Little Rooster is a trademark of Bantam Books,
a division of Bantam Doubleday Dell Publishing Group, Inc.

Series graphic design by Alex Jay/Studio J
Associate Editors: Gwendolyn Smith, Gillian Bucky

Special thanks to James A. Levine, Betsy Gould,
and Erin B. Gathrid.

Library of Congress Cataloging-in-Publication Data
Reit, Seymour.
Things that go : a traveling alphabet / by Seymour Reit ;
illustrated by Fulvio Testa.

p.   cm. — (Bank Street ready-to-read)
''*A Bantam little rooster book.*''
''*A Byron Preiss book.*''
Summary: Text and illustrations introduce vehicles
from A (Ambulance) to Z (Zeppelin).
ISBN 0-553-05856-8.— ISBN 0-553-34849-3 (pbk.)
1. Vehicles—Juvenile literature.   [1. Vehicles.   2. Alphabet.]
I. Testa, Fulvio, ill.   II. Title   III. Series.
TL147.R43   1990
629.04—dc20
[E]

89-37777   CIP   AC

Bantam Books are published by Bantam Books, a division of Bantam Doubleday
Dell Publishing Group, Inc. Its trademark, consisting of the words ''Bantam Books''
and the portrayal of a rooster, is Registered in U.S. Patent and Trademark Office
and in other countries. Marca Registrada. Bantam Books, 666 Fifth Avenue, New
York, New York 10103.

PRINTED IN THE UNITED STATES OF AMERICA

0 9 8 7 6 5 4 3 2 1

Bank Street Ready-to-Read™

Things That Go
A Traveling Alphabet

by Seymour Reit
Illustrated by Fulvio Testa

A Byron Preiss Book

A BANTAM LITTLE ROOSTER BOOK

NEW YORK · TORONTO · LONDON · SYDNEY · AUCKLAND

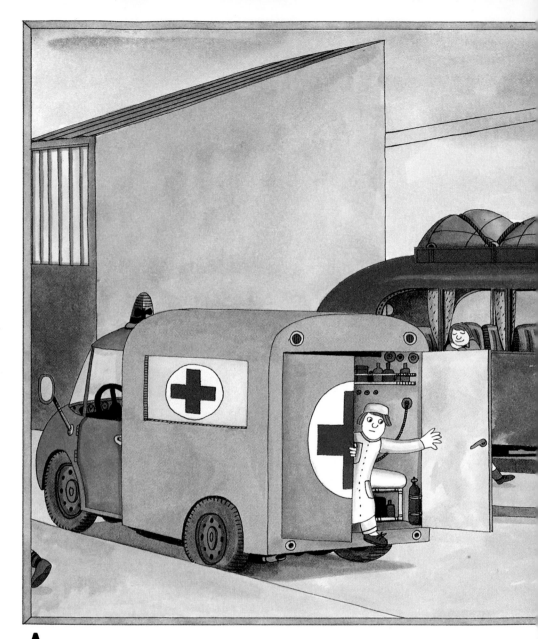

Aa **Ambulances** rush sick or hurt people to the hospital. Inside, an ambulance is like a little hospital room. *No time to lose*!

Bb A **bus** is made to carry many people. More people travel by bus than any other way.

Cc A **cable car** can take people where a car or truck can't go. Cable cars can go across rivers or up steep mountains. The car moves on a cable pulled by an engine. The biggest cable car in the world holds 121 people.

Dd A **dump truck** has to carry heavy loads. That's why it usually has six wheels instead of four. It can dump dirt, sand, gravel, or wood where it's needed. The part of the truck that tilts up to dump is called the bed.

Ee **Elevators** take people up and down
in stores and apartment houses.
They also carry workers and supplies
to the top of tall buildings.

Ff *Fire! Fire!* The **fire engine** rushes to put out a fire in a house or store. The siren tells you a fire engine is on the way. Some fire engines carry ladders and long hoses that can reach to the top of a tall building.

Gg **Garbage trucks** take away the trash.
At the back of the garbage truck, there's a big,
noisy compactor that smashes fat bags flat.
When the truck is full, the driver goes
to the dump and empties the trash.

Hh Helicopters can fly up, down, and sideways. They can stay in the air in one place. They have big spinning blades on top. Helicopters help guide traffic. They are also used for rescue work.

Ii The **ice-cream truck** is like a big freezer on wheels. It keeps the ice cream cold and hard. *I scream, you scream, we all scream for ice cream.*

Jj **Jet planes** travel from airport to airport. They carry people and baggage from place to place. Up, up, up . . . the jet soars, over the clouds and through the sky.

Kk **Kayaks** are canoes used by Eskimos in the cold North. They are often made of whalebone covered with sealskin. Kayaks fit around the rider's waist to keep icy water out. Eskimos use them to hunt seals and whales.

Ll The **lunar rover** was used
by the astronauts to explore the moon.
The rover looks like a jeep with satellite disks.
The lunar rover was left behind
on the moon for the next astronauts.

Mm Most **motorcycles** have two wheels and one seat. They look a lot like bicycles, but are bigger, heavier, and faster. Motorcycles are used for fun and for important jobs like patrolling the highways.

Nn A **nuclear submarine** can travel underwater twice as fast as other submarines. Navy submarines can go for nine years before the nuclear power runs out.

Submarines are also used for exploration.

Oo **Ocean liners** sail the sea from shore to shore like huge floating hotels. Passengers eat, sleep, and play as ocean liners sail across the water.

Pp **Pedalboats** glide slowly and quietly across a lake. They have no engine and need no gasoline. The pedalboat is like a bicycle that floats. It runs on pedal power!

Qq A **quarter boat** is a small boat that hangs from the quarterdeck of a big ship. Quarter boats are used for short trips. They can go places that a big ship can't. A quarter boat can come in handy as a lifeboat.

Rr **Racing cars** have large, smooth tires and light bodies. They are made in different shapes and are built for speed. This one is a model of an English racing car.

Ss **Spaceships** are used to carry people and equipment beyond the earth's atmosphere into space. The spaceship *Columbia* was our first space shuttle. It circled the earth in 110 minutes.

Tt *Toot! Toot!* Here comes a **train**! It runs on steel tracks. Its wheels sing *rackety-clack, rackety-clack!* Some trains have passenger cars. Some only carry freight. Others carry both people and freight.

Uu A **unicycle** has only one wheel and no handlebars. The rider steers by leaning. Getting on and off a unicycle is tricky! The tallest unicycle anyone has ever ridden is 101 feet high!

Vv **Vans** can look like cars or trucks.
Night and day, vans travel from factories
to stores, from house to house, over miles and
miles of roads. A moving van carries
all of a family's belongings to their new home.

Ww **Wagons** are pulled by animals, people, or motors. In pioneer days, people crossed the country in covered wagons. Today people cross the country in station wagons.

Xx A **xebec** is one of the oldest ships ever built. Xebecs were a favorite ship of the pirates! *Ahoy!*

Yy A **yacht** is a pleasure ship, made for fun. It moves by catching the wind in its sails.

Zz The **zeppelin** was an airship. It ran on a gas motor and used rudders for steering. The zeppelin looked like a modern blimp but was much larger.

Going from A to Z

An **a**mbulance rushes down the street.

A **b**us pulls up to the passenger stand.

A **c**able **c**ar slides by overhead.

A **d**ump truck dumps a load of sand.

An **e**levator squeaks going up and down.

A clanging **f**ire engine roars by.

A **g**arbage truck rumbles at the curb.

A **h**elicopter circles high in the sky.

The **i**ce cream truck plays a sweet-tooth song.

The **j**et plane swoops up with a whirring tune.

The **k**ayak skims the icy sea.

The **l**unar rover bumps along the moon.

A **m**otorcycle speeds down the road.

A **n**uclear submarine hides in a seaweed brake.

An **o**cean liner sails over the waves.

A **p**edalboat glides across the lake.

A **q**uarter boat hangs on the side of a ship.

A **r**acing car whizzes around the track.

A **s**pace **s**huttle orbits in outer space.

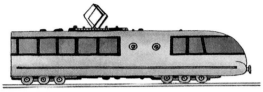

A **t**rain rides the rails singing rackety-clack.

The **u**nicycle goes on a single wheel.

The **v**an and the **w**agon haul goods for a crowd.

The **x**ebec and the **y**acht sail the seas.

The **z**eppelin floats silently through a cloud.

Seymour Reit, a Senior Editor for the Bank Street College Media Group, is a well-known cartoonist and author. He has written over sixty books for young readers, including *Voyage with Columbus* and *Behind Rebel Lines.* He originated the successful cartoon character Casper the Friendly Ghost, and was for years a regular contributor to *MAD* magazine. Mr. Reit's *Those Incredible Flying Machines* was selected as one of the year's ten best books for children by the *New York Times* in 1988.

Fulvio Testa was born in Verona, Italy, and studied architecture in Florence and Venice. Since he began writing and illustrating children's books in 1971, he has created more than 25 books, which have been published in 20 countries and translated into 13 languages. He is the recipient of numerous awards, including the Parents' Choice Award for *If You Take a Pencil.* Mr. Testa lives in Verona and in New York City.